TRAIL DRIVE

TRAIL DRIVE

Written and Illustrated by
JAMES RICE

PELICAN PUBLISHING COMPANY
Gretna 1996

*The word "Pelican" and the depiction of a pelican are trademarks
of Pelican Publishing Company, Inc., and are registered
in the U.S. Patent and Trademark Office.*

Library of Congress Cataloging-in-Publication Data

Rice, James, 1934-
    Trail drive / written and illustrated by James Rice.
        p.   cm.
    Summary: Texas Jack, the jackrabbit, describes the life of the cowboy during a trail
drive from the Texas plains to markets in the North after the Civil War.
    ISBN 1-56554-163-4 (hc)
    [1. Cattle drives—Fiction. 2. Cowboys—Fiction. 3. Texas—History—1846-1950—
Fiction.] I. Title.
PZ7.R3634Tr 1996
[E]—dc20
                                                                    96-23057
                                                                       CIP
                                                                       AC

Printed in Singapore

Published by Pelican Publishing Company, Inc.
1101 Monroe Street, Gretna, Louisiana 70053

TRAIL DRIVE

After the Civil War, literally millions of wild Longhorn cattle roamed the Southwest, particularly the brush country of South Texas.

Texas Jack sez having a herd of cattle was like having a pocketful of Confederate money. The nearest market was eight hundred to a thousand miles to the north.

The wild Longhorns were very difficult to work in the heavy brush. After they were out of the brush, *cabestros*, or trained oxen, helped control them.

Texas Jack sez you could spend a day riding through the thicket and the next two days pulling out the thorns and cactus spines.

Around a thousand or fifteen hundred cows were round-ed up and branded for each of those early trail drives. Much later, as many as five thousand might be in a single herd. A few old bulls and oxen were added to calm the frisky steers. Extra hands were hired to get the cattle off the home range.

Texas Jack sez them old Longhorns was real homebodies. They didn't like moving into new territory.

A herd spread out a mile or more on the trail. Scouts rode ahead to find the best route to water, point riders with oxen guided the herd, swing and flank riders kept the herd together, and drag riders brought up the rear.

Texas Jack sez young tenderfeet and them what found disfavor with the boss got to bring up the strays and eat dust on drag.

The wrangler drove the remuda* alongside the herd, far enough away to stay out of the dust.

*A herd of saddle horses

Texas Jack sez he best not get too far away or too scattered. A few Indians always kept an eye out to pick up any stragglers.

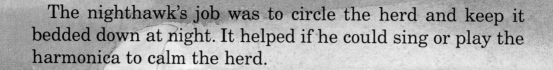

The nighthawk's job was to circle the herd and keep it bedded down at night. It helped if he could sing or play the harmonica to calm the herd.

Texas Jack sez a lot of trail bosses invested in a dozen or so French harps* before the drive. The music didn't have to be good, just so it was soothing.

*Another term for harmonicas

Cowboys expected two hot meals a day. The chuck wagon went ahead to the next campsite after breakfast to be ready with a hot supper. The cook was also doctor, barber, dentist, general repairman, and sometimes entertainer.

Texas Jack sez a good cook was expected to do pert near ever'thing extry that had to be did.

River crossings, especially in high water, were a real hazard. The trouble usually started when a cow tried to turn back in midstream, causing a mill. Good point men and a few good "swimmers" were invaluable in leading the stock across.

Texas Jack sez a lot of good cowboys went down and didn't come up trying to straighten out a mill.

Stampedes, especially at night, were the scariest things on the trail. The only cures were to let the cows run it out or turn them into a mill or tight circle.

Texas Jack sez night stampedes were usually caused by thunderstorms but pert near any disturbance could set off a restless herd.

Indians north of Texas often stopped the drive, demanding a toll to pass through their lands. A few drovers refused to pay, sometimes at the price of having their herd stampeded.

Texas Jack sez you couldn't really blame the Indians for wanting their due. The big herds would trample or graze down the Indians' pastures and farms and sometimes lure away their cattle.

Farther north they were often halted by local farmers or ranchers. The Longhorns carried ticks that spread Spanish fever to northern herds.

Texas Jack sez them tough Longhorns was immune to just about ever'thing, including Spanish fever.

Some trail bosses chose to detour to the east, where they were held up by hillbilly Jayhawkers who sometimes stole their herds.

Texas Jack sez them Jayhawkers claimed to be still fighting the Civil War but most were just plain hard cases looking for an excuse to plunder and go their outlaw ways.

Most trail drives eventually reached their goal: the market at the beginning of the railroad. Later on, the shipping center moved west from Kansas City, Missouri to Abilene, Kansas.

Texas Jack sez the smart cowboys put some wages aside for winter, but quite a few spent them celebrating on the town for several nights and wound up riding the grub line, broke till next season.

A few hands had winter work back at the main ranch.
Some did maintenance work; others manned the line camps
at the edge of the northern spreads to keep the cows from
drifting too far in winter.

Texas Jack sez there was nothing lonelier than being in a cold winter line camp, keeping an eye on a wandering herd.

Cowboying was a young man's job. A man was old and worn out by age forty, if he lived that long through the exposure to the elements and other hazards of the job.

Texas Jack sez it was hard, dangerous work with low pay but most cowboys wouldn't change their way of life for anything else.